TALES OF THE SUPERNATURAL

Witches and Warlocks

TALES OF THE SUPERNATURAL

Witches and Warlocks

by David Oakden

ROURKE PUBLICATIONS, INC.
Windermere, Florida 32786

Library of Congress Cataloging in Publication Data

Oakden, David, 1947-
  Witches & warlocks.

  (Tales of the supernatural)
  Summary: A collection of tales of persons whose
lives have been changed by contact with the supernatural.
  1. Supernatural—Juvenile fiction.   2. Children's
stories, English. [1. Supernatural—Fiction.   2. Witchcraft—Fiction.   3. Short stories]   I. Title.
II. Title: Witches and warlocks.   III. Series.
PZ7.01017Wi   1982   [Fic]   82-10140
ISBN 0-86625-205-3   AACR2

CONTENTS

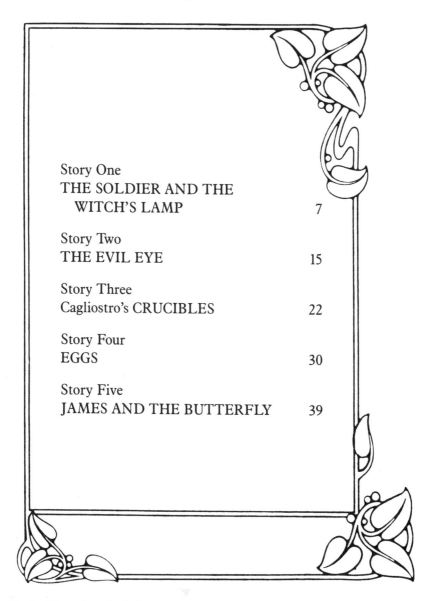

Enthralling tales of witches and warlocks (male witches). They make fascinating reading for young people interested in the occult.

Story One

The Soldier and the Witch's Lamp

On a stone by the side of the road was an old boot. Looking down at the boot was a tall soldier, and he was thinking. What he was thinking was that the boot on the stone was quite worn out, dropping to pieces, and surely not much use as a boot any longer.

"Boot," said the soldier, looking at it. "Boot, you're not much use." He thought again, and then looked down at the other boot. "And you're not much better. Both of you boots are done for!"

While this soldier was tall, he was not – as you may have guessed – very clever. In fact he was just the opposite: he was pretty stupid. After all he had been in the army for twenty years and had not risen above the rank of private. So at last the army had turned him out. Yes, he was turned out for being too stupid to rise above the rank of private!

"I hate boots," said the soldier, but all the same he took the worn-out boot off the stone and pulled it back on to his foot. Worn out it might be, but it was better than nothing. Then he looked around and was very pleased indeed to see that he was not far away from a cottage, white-painted and thatched. At the cottage door stood a tiny woman, throwing breadcrumbs to the birds.

"Hello there!" called the soldier.

"Hello to you," replied the tiny woman.

"Are you feeding the birds, then?" asked the soldier.

The woman looked at him, looked at the bread and then back again at him.

"What did you think I was doing, feeding fish?" she snapped.

The soldier shrugged his shoulders. "You don't happen to have a pair of boots you don't want, do you?" he asked.

The old woman thought, and as she thought her long crooked nose came down and her long sharp chin went up until the two almost met in front of her toothless mouth. She looked just like a witch. But then that is not surprising because that is just what she was, a really bad and wicked old witch!

"You're a good, strong fellow," she said at last. "I'll give you a pair of boots, a bed for the night and five sausages for your breakfast if you'll just do one little job for me."

The soldier put his head on one side and scratched it. "For six sausages," he said, "I'll do anything."

"Right," said the witch. "Six sausages, a pair of boots and a bed for the night. The job is to dig my back garden."

By the evening of the next day the job was done. The garden was dug, the soldier's stomach was full of sausage and his toes were twiddling comfortably in a pair of strong black boots. As he cleaned the spade, he used what little brain he had to think. After thinking awhile he went up to the little old woman with a suggestion.

"If I can stay another night and have ... er ... seven sausages for breakfast tomorrow morning I'll chop you enough firewood to last you through the winter."

"Right," said the old witch woman, "seven sausages. And the job is to chop enough wood to fill my wood-store."

By the time the sun was at its highest point the next day the job was done. The ground was littered with wood chippings, but the shed was full of good sticks and logs. The soldier enjoyed his sausages, and afterwards as he polished the blade of the axe he thought long and hard. Then he went to the old woman with a suggestion.

"If I stay here for ever, and you give me one more sausage every day, I'll do all your work for you."

The witch looked at him, and thought how stupid he was to ask for nothing more than sausages. He was so stupid, she thought, that he might be just the man to do a really difficult job for her, a job that she would never be able to do by herself.

"Right," she said. "Here's the next job. Climb down my old well over there and bring me up the blue lamp you'll find at the bottom of it. I'd go down myself but I'm too old and frail."

"A lamp?" said the soldier. Even he was surprised that a lamp, whatever its color, should be at the bottom of a well.

"I dropped it down one day by accident," said the witch.

The soldier said no more, but spat on his hands, grabbed the knotted rope of the well-bucket and slid down, down, down into the darkness below. Wet ferns brushed against his face, something nasty scuttled into a hole in the brickwork, but at last he reached the bottom. Looking up he could see a bright circle of light framing the face of the witch as she looked down eagerly from above.

"Have you got it?" cried out the witch.

"Wait a minute," he called up. "It's dark down here. If I could find it I'd be able to light it to help me find it, only if I could find it I shouldn't be needing to be looking, 'cos I should have found what I was looking for."

"Don't be so stupid. Keep looking!" came the witch's voice. At that very moment the soldier saw something glowing with a deep-blue light near his new boots. It was the lamp.

"Got it!" he called in triumph. "Pull me up!"

"Put the lamp in the bucket. I'll get that first and then I'll pull you up."

Well, the soldier may have been stupid, but he was not that stupid!

"Not likely," he said stoutly. "It's both of us together or neither of us."

"Then stay there!" yelled the cross witch in a dreadful voice, and she went back into her cottage and slammed the door.

Down at the bottom of the well the soldier sat and tried to work out how he could get back to the top of the well again. After ten minutes he had thought of nothing so he got out his pipe to have a smoke. He used the blue lamp to light the tobacco, but as he did so there was a puff of black smoke and in front of him appeared a little black dwarf!

"Bless me!" said the soldier. "Where were you hiding all this time?"

"I am the dwarf of the lamp," said the dwarf in a squeaky voice. "What can I bring you, master?"

The soldier scratched the back of his head with his pipe. "Can I have anything?" he asked at last.

"Anything, master."

"Then bring me eight sausages!"

And lo and behold, there on a plate in front of him were eight fat sausages, rich, brown and steaming hot.

"Anything else, master?" asked the dwarf in his squeaky voice.

The soldier spoke with his mouth full. "Yes, bring me some more saus.... No, wait. First of all, can you get me out of this well? If you can, do so, then bring that wretched old witch down here and leave her in my place. And when you've done all that you can get me a really big bag of gold."

All these things were done in a flash, and in a few moments the soldier creaked away down the road in his new boots, the lamp in his hand, leaving the witch sighing and crying at the bottom of the well. Before nightfall he was

sitting in the best bedroom of the best inn in the town and tucking into a huge meal of – well you can guess what he was eating!

On the next day he had such a pleasant thought. He looked at his new boots and then summoned the dwarf of the lamp. He remembered how he had served the King in the army for twenty years and had had nothing to show for it but a rotten pair of old boots. Now was his chance to get his own back.

"Has the King got a daughter?" he asked.

"Yes, master. Her beauty is spoken of by all who have seen her."

"Oh, blow her beauty," said the soldier. "Fetch her here tonight."

That night the sleeping Princess was plucked from her bed, rushed through the dark streets and plopped down in front of the soldier. She rubbed her eyes sleepily in amazement. She was even more amazed when she was handed a bucket of water and a scrubbing-brush and made to spend all night scrubbing the floor.

In the early morning the Princess was whisked back to her bed, and was soon sobbing out her story to the King, her father.

"Just look at my poor hands," she said, "all red and lumpy from that disgusting soap and water!"

"Never mind, dear." said the King. "I'll give you a bag of peas, so that if it happens again you can leave a trail of them behind you. Then we shall find where this madman lives!"

Well, that very night it *did* happen again. The Princess was whirled away by the dwarf and made to wash piles of dirty clothes and socks by the grinning soldier. On the way, however, she left behind her a trail of dried peas.

But the dwarf was no fool, even if his master was. As he took the Princess home he noticed the peas and guessed what had happened. So he spent the rest of the night scattering peas all over the town, down every street and up every road.

The next morning the King's guards, sent to follow the trail of peas, could see nothing but crowds of people gathering peas from everywhere. One or two pigeons were staggering about as well, unable to take off because their craws were stuffed so full. But as to where the Princess had spent the night there was no clue.

"Father!" wailed the young lady, holding out her water-wrinkled fingers. "Do something!"

"Don't worry, dear," said the King. "This time we'll have him for sure. When you get to his room tonight hide one of your shoes in the cupboard. We'll find it even if we have to take the whole town apart!"

That night the Princess spent hours in the soldier's room cooking sausages and onions, until her nose was red with the steam and her hair was straggling all over her face. The soldier thought what a great joke it was to get his own back on the King in this way.

But he was not so sure the next morning when four burly guardsmen with black moustaches found the Princess's shoe in his cupboard and hauled him off to prison at bayonet-point. He did not even have time to collect his things. All he had in his pockets was one gold ducat.

"Hello," said the jailer when he saw him, "you're just in time for the big show tomorrow."

"Big show?" said the soldier. "Will it be good?"

"Very good," said the jailer with a smile.

"Will I be able to go?"

"Oh, yes, you'll be going all right. There couldn't be a show at all if you weren't there!"

"How's that, then?" said the puzzled soldier.

"Why," said the jailer, holding his sides now with laughter, "you are the star of the show. You're going to do a very funny dance!"

13

"Me? A dance? What do you mean?"

"Don't you understand yet, you stupid man," said the jailer, putting his face very close to the soldier's. "You're going to dance on the end of a rope. They're going to hang you in the morning!"

The soldier sat down in his bare cell and thought hard. Then gradually an idea seeped into his brain and he fished out the gold ducat.

"If you fetch my belongings from the inn," he said to the jailer, "I will give you this gold piece." He drew his hand back as the jailer snatched. "Fetch the things first," he said craftily, "then I'll give you the gold."

He may have been stupid, but he was not that stupid.

Before long the jailer was back with the soldier's belongings and the blue lamp was in the soldier's hands. But the soldier did nothing until he was standing on the gallows the next day with a rope round his neck. Then he spoke to the King. "May I have a last request?" he said.

"Oh, I suppose so," said the King grudgingly.

"May I smoke my pipe for the last time?"

"If you like. But don't be long. I've more important things to do."

The soldier did not need long. One puff from the blue lamp and there stood the black dwarf.

"What is your wish, master?" said the midget.

"Kill, slay or otherwise exterminate most of these nasty people," said the soldier. "You can leave the King till last, but then chop him into three equal pieces!"

When he saw what was happening the King fell on his knees and cried for mercy, and since the soldier was quite kind, although he was stupid, he spared him. The soldier spared his life on condition that he gave him half his kingdom and the Princess for his wife. From that day on he lived in grand style, and he had as many sausages as he wanted for the rest of his life.

14

The Evil Eye

Certain people are said to be born with a strange power; the power to look into the future and say what is going to happen. It is as if they see a vision of things that are yet to come, though nothing that they do seems to be able to prevent those things from happening. This unusual gift is called "second sight," and it is said that the seventh child of a seventh child will always have this second sight.

Other people are said to have even greater powers. Not only do they have second sight to see into the future, but they can use their eyes in a terrible way. By staring hard at somebody they do not like, they can change the future – or so people say – and make terrible things happen. Such people are said to have the "Evil Eye", and many stories are told of witches, wizards and warlocks who are supposed to have this evil power.

One such story is about a poor Irish girl who earned her living by looking after the dairy at a large farm in the beautiful green county of Kerry. It took place a long time back, in fact about two hundred years ago, long before the days of cars and trains and aeroplanes. In those days there were only two ways for a man to get about the countryside: if he did not have a donkey or a horse then he had to walk.

This is what happened: One fine, hot summer day when the cows were standing knee-deep in the streams to cool themselves, Maureen, dairymaid at James O'Reilly's farm, was working in the stone-walled building where the morning's milk was cooling. This was the dairy. Wooden buckets and shining pans stood around on the flagged floor and a pair of swallows were flitting in and out of the open door to their nest up in the rafters.

Maureen sang as she worked. She was a happy, cheerful girl who lived with her widowed mother in a turf-roofed cottage, and every Sunday she went to the church close by. When autumn came she was to marry James, one of the farm-hands. The harvest looked as if it would be good. Autumn would not be long. Maureen's future looked bright and happy.

But as she worked and sang a shadow fell across the doorway. For some reason the swallows disappeared. Although the sun still shone, the air seemed suddenly colder.

Mary looked up from her work to see a young man standing at the door, watching her. He was tall, wore a battered green hat and had a straw in his mouth. His face was as brown as a berry and he carried himself well, as if he were used to much walking. Nevertheless, there was something odd about him, and his sudden, silent appearance startled Maureen so that she dropped a wooden pail with a clatter.

"It's a beautiful morning, mistress, to be sure," said the man.

His voice was light and clear. He would be a good singer, Maureen thought.

"So it is," she said in answer, nervously wiping her hands on her white dress. "Is it Mr O'Reilly you're looking for?"

The man did not answer her question. Instead he looked straight at her and said, "I have here a poem you will like. Listen."

So saying, he began to recite the poem in his clear voice. It was all about the far blue hills and the rushing streams that ran between them and down to the steep sea-cliffs. His words were strange and old-fashioned, but the poem was so beautiful that Maureen's eyes filled with tears as she remembered her own childhood and the happy time she

16

had then. Through the tears the man's figure seemed hazy – one minute filling the doorway, and the next looking small and stocky. His voice went on and on and she listened as if in a dream.

Suddenly the poem came to an end and Maureen came to with a start. She wiped her eye and looked at the man, who stood there smiling in an odd way. "Was it Mr O'Reilly you were after?" she said again.

The man still did not answer her question, but instead came nearer and stared into her face with his strange pale-blue eyes. He seemed to be thinking hard.

"You are a kind-looking girl, my dear," he said at last. "What is your name?"

"Maureen, but you must not come into the dairy, sir. Mr O'Reilly says no stranger must ever come in here – you see, it has to be kept spotless. . . ."

The man took no notice but continued to come nearer. "Maureen," he said, still looking at her, "I am going to ask you a favour. Give me just a cup or two of the fine creamy milk I can see here, and let me rest for a short while on that bench in the cool of the shade."

The girl was frightened. She had liked the man's poem but she certainly did not like the way he looked at her. She would have run away and out of the dairy but he was between her and the door. She started to tremble.

"I cannot, sir, really," she said in a frightened whisper. "I dare not. Mr O'Reilly wouldn't . . ."

"Give me milk! Give me rest!" said the man sharply, and now his eyes were as cold and as hard as winter ice.

"I dare not!" cried Maureen, regaining her voice, and in terror she began to call for help.

The man stood his ground, but a great scowl came over his face and to Maureen's horror those icy eyes seemed to get bigger and bigger. Her knees trembled and seemed as if they would give way. The dairy began to sway around her.

17

Wherever she looked she could see nothing but those huge staring eyes.

Suddenly, outside, a dog barked. In a trice the man had gone, and Maureen sank senseless to the floor.

By the time help arrived in the dairy the man had disappeared from sight. The anxious farmer and his wife cooled Maureen's hot brow with cold cloths, so that gradually she came to her senses again. But she could not speak and her face was blank and expressionless.

"What happened, girl?" asked Mr O'Reilly. "Why did you call for help?"

Mrs O'Reilly helped Maureen to her feet, and then the girl shook off the helping hand and moved to the doorway, still without speaking. There she stood, gazing across the green fields. The others strained their eyes to see what she was looking at. On the other side of the small stream, close to the edge of the wood, they could just make out what seemed to be the figure of a man, his face turned towards them. But even as they glimpsed him he vanished into the trees and out of sight.

Almost immediately Maureen seemed to be better and turned to her work again as if nothing had happened. But she still did not speak, and moved as if in a trance, so Mr O'Reilly told James to stay close at hand and not to let the girl out of his sight.

It was a good job he did so, too. All at once, as if at a signal, Maureen dropped a can and started to move, in a dreamy sort of way as if sleep-walking, out of the door again. Then she headed at a brisk pace across the fields towards the wood. James strained his eyes and again he thought he could see the figure of a man standing within the fringe of trees, staring at the farm.

He raised the alarm and he and the farmer, followed by Mrs O'Reilly and one of the cow-hands, raced after the girl, who it seemed was being called by someone who was yet out of sight. As the girl's pace quickened, the figure of a man appeared again, this time quite clearly. He was beckoning her towards him and even at that distance the followers could see his eyes gleaming with a cold light.

"Stop, Maureen! Stop!" roared James, plunging through the long grass.

At the sound of his voice the man seemed to take fright, for he dropped his beckoning hands and melted into the shadows of the trees. At that moment Maureen also reached the trees and then disappeared.

By the time the others, now out of breath, reached the edge of the woods, there was no sign of either the girl or the man. Despairingly they called and yelled Maureen's name again and again. There was no answer. They stood quite still, but could hear nothing. Even the birds had stopped singing. There was a deathly silence as if the whole world were waiting for something to happen.

James leant on a tree in weariness and despair. Then suddenly he saw something he had failed to notice before: a piece of paper jammed into the broken end of a branch. Obviously it had been pushed there on purpose.

The young man reached up and took the paper off the branch. He smoothed it out and looked at it and, even as he did so, they heard a faint cry not far away. They ran in the direction from which it had come to find Maureen standing in an open clearing. She was looking around her in astonishment. "Where am I?" she asked in her normal voice, and went over to James, apparently pleased to see him. "What am I doing here? Why are we all in the woods? What's been going on?"

They led her gently out of the wood, and there Mr O'Reilly tried to explain what had happened. "It was as if you were under the spell of someone very wicked," he said gently. "I suspect you'd had the Evil Eye put on you. Can you not remember anything at all, my dear?"

Maureen told them of the strange young man's visit to the dairy, but her story ended at the point where she had fainted when the dog had barked. "But how did he get me to go out to the woods?" she said in a puzzled tone of voice.

Just then James, who had been looking at the piece of paper which he had found, gave a cry of surprise. "Hey, look here!" he said. "This must have been the spell that bewitched Maureen. Look at it. I reckon that the spell was broken when I took the paper off the tree!"

The others gathered round the paper to see, roughly printed, five strange words arranged in a square:

```
S A T O R
A R E P O
T E N E T
O P E R A
R O T A S
```

"What does it all mean?" said Maureen.

"That I cannot tell," replied James. "But it is certainly magic, for whichever way you read it, forwards, backwards, up or down, the words always read the same. I think that it is a very powerful spell, and that you must be the luckiest girl alive!"

Well, no doubt James was right. In any case he and Maureen were married when the harvest was safely in, and the young man was never seen again in that neighbourhood. Maureen became the mother of five lovely children and James, by hard work, got a farm of his own with a good house. And on winter evenings the whole family would sit round the fire while Maureen retold the strange story of the young man with the ice-blue eyes and the beautiful poem and the magic word-square.

Story Three

Cagliostro's Crucibles

A small coach stopped outside an inn near the town of Cracow in Poland. As the innkeeper and several servants hurried out to greet their guests, the coach door opened and down stepped a man in a long and magnificent blue coat.

The man spoke shortly to the servants and then handed a small locked wooden box to the innkeeper. "Here," he said in good Polish but with a foreign accent. "Guard this box with your life, landlord."

The landlord peered curiously at the precious box. "Certainly, my lord," he said. "But whose name shall I write on the label?"

The man drew a silk handkerchief from the tail-pocket of his coat, flourished it in the air and then blew his nose with a. blast like a trumpet. "My name is Cagliostro," he announced. "The Count of Cagliostro. Write the label so."

Now the name of Cagliostro had been heard before, even in this remote area. It was the name of a man who, so rumour had it, was in league with the devil himself; a man who could work magic, a man who could make spells, a man it was very wise to keep on the right side of!

Word soon got round the neighbourhood that the famous Count of Cagliostro was staying at the inn, and more than one local Nosy Parker stopped by that evening to peer into the private room where the Count was having his meal. Eyes grew round as they took in the full powdered wig, the gold braid on the coat, the fine lace frothing out of the cuffs and the gold buckles on the shoes. Here was a man of wealth, here was a real nobleman.

Then to everyone's great surprise there was a rumble of wheels and another coach drew up at the door. The man who got out this time was, however, well known to everybody as the owner of a fine house and estate not half a day's ride away. He was known to be exceedingly rich, though it was rumoured that he was by no means clever. At any rate here he was, and he and Cagliostro shut the door of the private room behind them and talked together in low voices for a long, long time.

Nobody could imagine why the two men had met and talked so secretively, but the next day there were more surprises still.

The Count rose early, breakfasted well on chops and beer, and then started giving a series of orders.

"I need the use of one of your stables, landlord," he said.

The landlord at first looked doubtful. His stables were full of horses. But a black look from the Count, and a piece of gold slipped into his hand, soon made him change his mind and bob his head.

"Yes, Count, of course, Count, certainly, my lord, anything you say, Count."

"One of your servants can go to the nearest blacksmith and ask him to come and see me. On the way back he can find a man who can build with bricks. While he is doing that another servant can fetch a supply of charcoal and firewood. Send a third into Cracow for two small china crucibles. Understand?"

"Yes, Count. Er . . . no, Count. I do not know what a loosible is."

"Crucible, crucible, idiot! Crucibles are small china dishes made to withstand great heat. Crucibles! I must have two and they must be the same size and look the same. Now do you understand?"

23

"Yes, Count, but why . . . ?"

But Cagliostro turned his back and walked away.

There was a great deal of activity that day and by evening, inside the end stable of the inn-yard, there was a small furnace. This had been made by the builder under the directions of the blacksmith. A small but hot fire of charcoal was burning in it and there was enough wood close by to keep it going for a very long time. The Count, handkerchief to his nose to keep away the stable smell, inspected the work and was satisfied. Money changed hands and the Count and his servant were finally alone in the stable.

"Up there?" asked the servant, pointing to a tiny loft in a dark corner of the stable. The loft was used for storing hay and was full to bulging-point. The Count looked at the loft and nodded. No more was said.

That night the coach arrived again, and this time there were three men in it, all muffled in cloaks and wearing big hats. Cagliostro went out to greet them, bearing in his hands a small locked box. "My dear Frederick," he said to the man who had been with him before. "Introduce me to your friends."

"Ah, yes," said Frederick. "This is . . . er . . . William and this . . . er . . . er . . . this is Stanislas. They would prefer it if their other names and titles were not known, even to you."

Cagliostro smiled faintly. "I care not who they are, if the truth be told. All I ask is that they bear witness to my curious powers. The rewards shall be theirs, not mine. I have more money than I know what to do with already!"

"Where . . . er . . . how . . . ?" stammered the man called Frederick.

Cagliostro raised the silk handkerchief to his nose and sniffed delicately. "In the stable, my dear sir, I am afraid. In the stable. But never mind, stable or palace, gold is gold, eh?"

The others looked round nervously and pulled their coat collars up at the mention of gold, but Cagliostro was already leading the way firmly over the cobbles and into the stable

24

where the furnace was lit and glowing. It was hot, dark and smoky inside the low building, and the red light from the furnace cast queer leggy shadows on the raftered ceiling and beamed walls.

Near the surface, on a bench, stood a small white crucible. Cagliostro handed it to Frederick, who examined it and passed it to the others. An ostler from the inn, standing by the furnace, gave an experimental press on the bellows, at which flames began to roar like demons. Outside it began to rain.

"Empty?" asked the Count with a slight smile. The others nodded. "Then did you bring the mercury?"

Frederick produced a stone jar and carefully removed the cork. Inside a dull, silvery metal flopped about. Carefully the jar was tilted over the crucible until the metal ran out and half filled it. Then Cagliostro began his work.

First he examined the mercury and nodded to himself as if satisfied that it was pure. Then he unlocked the small wooden box and peered inside it. One by one he fetched out bottles and phials and packets. He added to the mercury a pinch of this, a drop of this, a shake of that and two or three of those. As he added to the mixture he began to chant in a low voice – too low for the others to catch the words, even though they strained their ears. The drumming of the rain on the roof was loud and regular.

At last Cagliostro seemed satisfied. He drew a small wand from his pocket and stirred the mixture in the crucible once, twice, thrice. Then he threw a handful of yellow powder on to the flames of the furnace. The fire burned blue and orange, the ostler pumped away at the bellows as if the devil himself were standing behind him. The glow reflected in the sweating faces of the eager men, and flickered over the face of Cagliostro – upon his heavy pointed eyebrows, high cheek-bones and small beard. Perhaps he was smiling; certainly there was a twisted edge to his thin mouth.

A distant rumble of thunder echoed through the stable

and, as if prompted by that sound, the Count seized the crucible in a pair of heavy tongs and set it in the centre of the furnace. Then he stood back and threw the tongs with a clatter into the corner of the room. "All done," he said. "Now, gentlemen, we will lock the door and go over to the inn for wine to help pass the time. Then, in about three hours, there will ... well, you shall see, you shall see!"

The ostler gave a last pump to the bellows and went out. Frederick took a heavy lock and chain from his pocket and sent all the others out. Then he tested the iron bars on the window: they were set in the brickwork and were far too close together to allow anyone to crawl between them. He pulled the door to behind him as he went out, slammed the hasp across and locked the stable, leaving the furnace and the crucible and the queer shadows to themselves.

There was a storm that night more violent than any man could remember. Inside the inn four men sat and drank in a private room in almost total silence. A rickety old clock on the mantelshelf slowly ticked away. Outside, the thunder roared and flashes of lightning lit the puddled yard, showing clearly the new lock gleaming on its chain at the stable door. Frederick sat on a tall chair at the window gazing out at the rain. From his seat he could see both the door and the window of the stable – he was determined to see that nobody got in.

The clock wheezed the hour once more and the three men rose: Cagliostro slowly finishing his drink and not hurrying, the others fumbling at the latch and splashing hastily across the steaming yard in their eagerness to reach the stable.

Frederick unlocked the door, threw back the hasp and went in. Holding the others back for a second he pointed at the floor. It was bone-dry – no one could have reached the stable on such a night with dry feet. No one had come in. The men approached the furnace which was crackling as it cooled down.

Cagliostro raised his handkerchief to his nose and said, "Well, well, my dear Frederick, go ahead. There are the tongs. Pick out the crucible."

Frederick's hands trembled as he reached into the furnace with the tongs and carefully lifted out the crucible. The others peered into the shallow dish and at first were disappointed, for all they could see was a layer of black ash and dust.

Then Cagliostro pushed them out of the way, seized the tongs and turned the crucible upside-down on the sandy floor with a good thump. As he lifted the crucible off again, a dome-shaped piece of dull yellow metal was left behind on the floor. Cautiously, Frederick reached down and scratched the metal with the blade of his knife. There was no need to do more. There was no doubt about what lay at their feet. They had left behind them in the locked room a crucible full of mercury and chemicals and had come back to a crucible full of pure, solid gold!

William, Stanislas and Frederick hugged themselves in their delight and shook Cagliostro's hands warmly. Then bargains began to be struck. The Count was handed great sums of money in large, heavy bags and in return he handed over a piece of paper with writing on it and a list of strangely named powders and liquids.

"Gentlemen," said Cagliostro at last, "I have shown you how to change the laws of nature. If you now make sure that you choose the finest ingredients and keep your crucibles clean, nothing is likely to go wrong. You will all be as rich as King Midas." He bowed low and then went out into the inn, leaving the other three to their imaginations.

Early next morning Cagliostro and his servant breakfasted well, paid the bill and left by the same small coach that had brought them. The innkeeper, for his part, was well pleased to see him go, for he was quite sure that he had been entertaining a very evil man: "It was his eyes, sort of queer they were – and all those odd goings-on in the stable! And then there was

28

that thunderstorm, coming suddenly. And what about those other fellows, all wrapped up as if nobody had to see them? Aye, a right evil man if you ask me!"

Not too far away there were three other men who also thought badly of Cagliostro. Frederick and his friends toiled away for the next few days and nights round a hot furnace, getting angrier and angrier. However pure the chemicals and however clean their crucibles, all they ever got out after heating them in the furnace were cracked crucibles and hot mercury!

At last, in a rage, they drove back to the inn. There they found the landlord standing in the end stable and grumbling. "I've got to get a builder in now to move that dratted furnace," he was saying. He turned and saw his three visitors. "Oh, and gentlemen, the Count must have left this behind – it was up in the little hayloft there. Though what anyone wanted to go up there for, I shall never know – made quite a little hidy-hole in the hay, though, somebody has."

Frederick took what the landlord was holding out and silently showed it to the others. All became very clear, for what he was holding was a second crucible, a twin of the one which had held gold. But this one had never held gold. All it contained were a few drops of mercury and a mess of coloured powders!

Story Four

Eggs

Down the hill and into the tiny village of Shippens strode a tall man. His hair and beard were as black as the wisps of wool left by the fell sheep on the sharp rocks of the dry stone walls. A long black cloak hung from his bony shoulders and covered him completely, right down to the ragged hose clinging round his thin ankles. As he walked he chanted an odd sort of song on three notes. The words were lost in the wind but they sounded low and mournful.

It was getting on for midday. Summer had been a long time coming that year, but for the last week or so there had been nothing but blazing sunshine and a dry easterly wind. The sun had dried the winter street-mud into dust, and the wind was now whirling this dust round the backs of the half-timbered cottages. Somewhere a cross housewife slammed a lattice window shut. A white hen cackled in alarm and scuttled past the tall man's legs.

The man raised his thick wooden staff and aimed a quick blow at the running hen, but it had gone. With a sigh he sank down on a high doorstep to rest.

After a few minutes he took a careful look up and down the street. Nobody was about. Swiftly he reached underneath his cloak and drew out a tall, narrow-brimmed black hat with a silvery band round its rim. Then he stood up and slipped the cloak from his shoulders. With a deft snap of his wrists he reversed the cloak and in a flash it was back on his shoulders – but now, instead of being plain black, it was covered with golden stars and crescent moons and odd Eastern hieroglyphics.

Next he did a very strange thing. He lifted up his staff and took a close look at one end of it. Then he raised it to his long nose and sniffed at it. Finally he held it up to his ear, shook it gently and smiled.

He was satisfied with all that he had done. Everything was ready. Slowly he got to his feet again, pulled the tall hat on to his head and began to call out in a high-pitched voice, "People of Shippens! People of Shippens!"

Somewhere a dog barked. Two small scruffy children appeared from round a corner and approached him with curiosity. One or two faces appeared in windows and then went away again. The dog suddenly stopped barking with a yelp as a foot caught it in the ribs.

The man lifted up his voice and called again, "People of Shippens!"

Two or three women now came out of their front doors, shading their eyes against the glare of the sunlight. A large whiskery man in a leather apron, carrying a short hammer, came out of the forge farther up the street. One by one the villagers came to the calls, and stood looking at this odd man in the peculiar clothes who was standing there shouting.

"People of Shippens!" called the man again. "I am here!"

"So we see," said a fat woman, folding her arms comfortably. "But now that you're here, who are you?"

The man raised his long staff and lowered it, pointed a dirty finger-nail at the signs on his cloak and said, "My name is Mercurio and I am a wizard!"

The little crowd drew back slightly, and one or two even crossed themselves. A small child, sensing fear, began to cry, but was hushed by its mother.

At length the blacksmith spoke. "Wizard? Wizard?

You don't look much like a wizard to me! You look more like an old fool to me!"

A little laugh came from the crowd and the feeling of fear vanished.

"Go on then," said a woman, suddenly daring, "if you're a wizard, do us some magic."

Mercurio looked thoughtful. Then he bent his head, muttered some strange words, waved his staff round in a circle and then straightened up again. "There you are," he said. "There's some magic for you."

"Where? Where? What has he done? What is it?" said the little crowd, looking round doubtfully. Nothing appeared to have changed.

"I have made a spell," said the wizard, "which has sent that thunderstorm packing. It won't rain today now."

"What thunderstorm?" said a young man suspiciously. "I saw no clouds!"

"My eyes are older but stronger than yours, young man. Had you really not noticed the gathering storm over the church tower? It was there, I can assure you, until my spell drove it away."

Some believed him. Others nodded wisely to each other, tapped their foreheads and began to drift away.

"Stay!" called Mercurio. "See, I will give these good people who believe me one of my special earthquake pills." And he handed to each one a small white pill.

"Will it really keep earthquakes away?" asked a youth.

The wizard tossed a pill up into the air, caught it neatly in his mouth and swallowed hugely. "My good man, I have taken one of these every day of my life, ever since my grandfather took the recipe for them from the hand of a dying Turkish Grand Wizard. Is it not obvious that I have never been in an earthquake? Of course they work. Have faith, sir, have faith!"

"What do you want here?" said the smith, shouldering his hammer.

"Want? Want of you? Why, nothing. Nothing at all. It would be better if you asked what I could do for you!"

Since nobody said anything, the man eased the sweat from under the rim of his tall hat and went on. His voice took on a new tone now as if, eyes half closed, he was seeing into the future. "I foresee many things happening in Shippens. I see things good and I see things bad. I see strangers coming into the village, strangers that you do not want."

"You're one of them!" called a boy with red hair, and the little crowd laughed.

The man swiftly reached under his cloak and then leaned down and patted the little boy on the head, smiling. "I see a boy whose hair is now the colour of the rising sun. That hair will begin to turn white before he is many hours older. Those who mock true wizards must suffer for it."

The boy tugged down a forelock of his hair and squinted at it with a worried frown. It was still fiery red and he smiled scornfully.

"Get on with it," said the smith angrily.

The wizard reached under his cloak again and this time produced a wooden box, gaudily painted and covered with cabalistic signs. "See then, friends. I have travelled many miles to give you these pills. Last week, as I slept in the palace of the Great Cham of China, I dreamed, and in that dream I saw this village, the village of Shippens. In my dream it was a day like today and you were going about your business. Suddenly there was a terrible outcry. A man came rushing down the street calling out bad news. In my dream I saw him telling you that an awful disease had struck the sheep up on the fellside and that they were all dying – a disease that spread from sheep to sheep and from farm to farm, until all the sheep for miles around were dead or dying. I saw all this, I tell you, in my dream."

The crowd murmured and began to look anxious, but the smith was scornful. "Dreams! Dreams!" he said. "Our

33

sheep are all well. Why should we believe the words of a madman who has bad dreams? And what could we do even if we did believe you?"

The wizard tapped the box. "There is a cure," he said. "This box holds enough pills to give one to every sheep you own. Give them immediately and the disease will be stopped before it starts."

"What do you want for your magic pills, then?" said a farmer. "That is, how much should we have to pay to buy them if we wanted to buy them, which we don't."

The crowd laughed again at the man's mocking words.

"I want no more than they are worth. Give me food and shelter for the night. Give me some new clothes to replace these old ones. Give me just a little money to take me on my way. That is all!"

"All?" laughed the farmer. "We are to give you food, clothing and shelter – not forgetting some money – and you give us some worthless pills which will keep away a disease we are never likely to see! That's all, is it?"

The crowd began to move away.

But Mercurio raised his staff. "Stop!" he called in a loud voice. "I must try to do the good I came to do. I will have to try to prove my powers to you. Let me see. Yes, I will prove them to you in three ways."

The crowd hesitated, and then someone said, "Well, go on then, prove something."

The wizard again held up his staff. "First," he said, "there is a dead sheep on the fellside." He pointed up at the hills he had crossed that morning. "There are no marks on its body and it lies in the open, well away from any rocks or cliffs, so it could not have fallen. It is dead of the disease I told you about. Proof number one."

A boy ran out of the village in the direction the wizard had indicated.

"Second," went on Mercurio, "there is that boy who was so rude to me. Even now he is losing the redness of his hair. He will wash it to try to keep it red, but it is already beginning to turn white. Proof number two."

The boy grabbed at his hair and began to cry. It still looked red, but his mother, with a fierce look at the wizard, got hold of her son by the scruff of the neck and dragged him off to the village pump. Almost immediately the crowd heard the boy scream as the cold water hit the back of his neck, and then they heard the woman call out in a frightened voice, "It's true! It's true! There is a patch of white hair on the top of his poor little head!"

The boy's howls mingled with the chattering of the crowd, and just at that moment the lad who had been sent to find the dead sheep came running back down the street. He was gasping for breath. "It's true!" he said, puffing. "There is a dead sheep, one of Paul's ewes, lying on the fellside as if asleep. But it's not sleeping, it's as dead as stone!"

Then Mercurio raised his staff yet again. "Two proofs of my powers, you foolish people. Now I will show you a third, and prove this time that I can live without help from anyone. I shall never starve. I can make food by my magic powers!"

At this statement everybody gasped. Then at the wizard's orders a small fire of sticks was kindled in the very middle of the village street. A woman ran into her cottage and came out with a large black pan. Somebody else flattened the fire and put the empty pan on it.

The little crowd pressed closer to see. Then the wizard, lifted his eyes to the skies, began to speak strange words and phrases. The words sounded foreign, but were musical, and as they came from the wizard's mouth a strange thing happened.

All the time he had been chanting his spell, Mercurio had been using the end of his staff to stir the empty pan

36

on the fire. Nothing else had happened, but all at once there was a faint sizzling sound and a smell of hot fat drifted through the air!

The sizzling got louder and the people craned their necks to see into the pan. And now their noses and their eyes told them the same marvellous thing: what had been an empty pan was now a pan of delicious, steaming, bubbling and mouth-watering scrambled eggs!

Mercurio stopped stirring and lifted the pan from the fire. He held it up. "Abracadabra!" he said. "Proof number three!"

Well, after that, the wizard's pills were seen by everybody as being very necessary. The wooden box was soon empty and eager farmers were dashing off up the fells to prise open their sheep's jaws and thrust round white tablets down their throats. Back in the village the wizard was given a very good meal, a new suit of clothes and a pocketful of money. As evening fell he was taken into one of the cottages where he spent a restful night on the softest feather bed in the village.

As the sun rose next morning Mercurio said goodbye and left the village. Staff in hand he said farewell to the smiling people and was soon striding through the dewy grass towards the next town.

However, once he was out of sight of the village he stopped and sat down at the side of the track. Off came his tall hat, off came his spangled cloak to turn again into an ordinary black one. He opened his bag and peered inside, smiling. "A pleasant village," he said to himself, "but very simple people. It was a good job I found that dead sheep and had the sense to drag it well away from the rocks it had fallen off. Broken neck probably." He smiled at the memory. "I hope that wretch of a boy has a few nightmares, too, before his head turns red again. Funny how that powdered bleach doesn't work until it gets wet. I must remember to visit old Issacs in York and get a new supply from him."

For a minute or two Mercurio sat and rested, reminding himself also of the need to get a new supply of sugar pills the next time he was in a town. Then he picked up his staff, turned it upside-down and looked at the end. He could see what the villagers had not spotted; that what appeared to be solid wood was in fact hollowed out for about a foot of its length. The wizard poked his finger into the hollow, smelt it, made a face and wiped at it with a bit of old rag.

That done he fetched out of his bag six duck's eggs, given to him the night before by one of the sheep-farmers, and a small wooden box of dripping. One by one he broke the eggs and poured them, yolks, white and all into the hollow staff. Then he got a lump of the dripping and sealed the end up with it, smoothing it round with his fingers until nobody could tell that the staff had anything hidden inside it. It looked, at both ends, like a solid piece of wood.

And so he was ready to go on. He stood up and sniffed the air. His new clothes felt good and comfortable. There was a pleasant sound of jingling coins in his pocket. His stomach was full of a good breakfast. "What a lovely day!" said Mercurio happily. "I fancy a good meal of scrambled eggs when I get to the next village."

James
and the Butterfly

James Meldrake had never been to school. All that he knew, he had learned from his father and mother, and by watching how the changing seasons brought different work to the family farm. Therefore, by the time he was a grown man, he knew all there was to know about how to breed and rear sheep. He knew how to yoke oxen to the plough and how to plough a first furrow as straight as the willow wands he used to mark it out with; he knew how to flail and winnow the chaff from the wheat; he knew how to milk and to turn the milk into cheese and butter.

James might not have been able to read and write – few could in his time – but he was an excellent farmer.

When his parents died James took over the family farm, and he and his wife, Susan, were very happy there in spite of knowing that they would never be rich. As the years went by they had a daughter, followed by a son, and for a time it seemed that nothing could spoil their happiness.

But then something happened that threatened their good life.

It all began like this. James was out early one fine May morning walking through his top meadow. Carrying a long ash-stick, he was on his way to the edge of his fields. At this point there was a curious round hill with a shallow cave slanting into its grassy side. The cave was used only by jackdaws in the nesting season, by sheep when it snowed, and by the occasional traveller caught out in a storm. However, on the previous evening, just as the sun had been setting, his son William had reported seeing something moving up there by the cave. "Perhaps it's a wolf, Father," he had said excitedly, his blue eyes shining at the thought of an adventure. He was a daring lad, and even though he was only eight years old he was strong and could already hit a target at twenty paces with his father's yew bow.

"Hasn't been a wolf around here for twenty years, son," James had replied. "It's more likely to be some poor fellow creature resting from a long journey."

As he drew near to the cave James stopped, and then he walked on warily. A wisp of wood-smoke was spiralling upwards from a small camp-fire and a smell of fresh mutton stew came from a blackened cooking-pot. The farmer's face grew dark as he saw what looked like the remains of a young lamb lying nearby, and a blood-stained fleece hanging over a bush. He quickened his pace and at the entrance to the cave, stooped down to peer in.

"Come out of there, whoever you are!" he called fiercely. "Let me have a look at whoever it is goes around stealing and eating other people's lambs!"

But James was in for a surprise, for it was not a man but an old woman in a long dark dress who came hobbling out of the cave. The black boots she was wearing were cracked and she had a dirty kerchief tied round her neck. Her skin was rough and leathery, not brown as it would have been if she had lived an outdoor life, but grey and wrinkled and unhealthy looking. Strangest of all were her eyes, for one was brown and crafty-looking while the other was almost white with pale grey lashes.

"Who are you?" asked James, grasping his ash-stick nervously and taking a pace backwards. There was something about this woman that made him uneasy.

The woman brushed a strand of lank hair from her face

40

and shaded her eyes to look up at the tall man in front of her. "Big, ain't you?" she said in a husky voice. "Strong, ain't you?"

"Who are you?" said James, afraid of the two peculiar eyes peering at him.

"Rich farmers like you, big strong men, like to hurt poor old women like me who do them no harm. Don't you, eh?"

James forgot his fear and his face grew angry. "I'm not rich and I haven't hurt you. But by rights I ought to turn you over to the magistrate for killing one of my lambs."

The old woman continued to look straight at him. Her strange white eye looked blank, and yet at the same time it seemed to see through him.

"Was the lamb yours? Or did I buy it at the market over Shelstone way? Or perhaps I was given it by a kinder farmer than you?"

James hesitated. He did not want to accuse the old woman unjustly. There was indeed no proof that the dead lamb had been one of his flock. He poked at the remains of the lamb with his stick.

"That's as maybe," he said at last. "But you are still on my land. Pack up your belongings. I'm going to look at a fence just round the other side of the hill, and when I come back I'll expect to find that you have gone."

He walked off round the hill, glad to be away from the strange woman. There really was a hole in the fence and he spent a few minutes dragging brambles and thorn-branches across the gap. Wisps of wool had caught on thorns near the hole and he wondered if any of his sheep would be missing then it came to counting-time.

When he returned to the cave there was no sign of the old woman. He shaded his eyes and looked around to see which way she had gone. From where he stood he could see for miles in all directions, and he expected to catch sight of her hobbling away in her dark clothes. But there was no sign of her. She seemed to have vanished into thin air. The

41

only living creature anywhere near was a grey and white spotted butterfly resting on a rock. That's odd, thought James. I don't see how she can have disappeared so quickly.

But she certainly had gone and James saw no more of her that day.

As he and his wife sat at supper that evening James told her what had happened up by the cave. "And on my way home," he said, "I had a very lucky escape. You remember that last year I dug an animal-trap near the forest path – that wild boar was being a nuisance. Well of course I know where it is and keep well away, but just as I was going past it today a grey and white butterfly flew straight out of a bush into my eyes. It almost made me trip over a fallen branch, and if I had done so I could easily have fallen head first into that boar-trap. I wouldn't like to think what might have happened to me if I'd tripped on to those sharpened stakes at the bottom of the pit!" He shuddered at the thought.

The boy William had been listening. "I've never seen a butterfly that colour around here, Father," he said. "I must go and look for it."

Strangely enough, from that day onwards nothing seemed to go right for James and his family. First of all one of his best cows stopped giving milk – her udder became as dry as if she had never given any. That had never happened before.

Then a few days later, out of a clear blue sky, lightning struck an old elm tree near the farm buildings. A heavy branch smashed down on to the stable, sending chunks of stone and slate crashing about the heads of the horses inside. Fortunately none of them was injured badly, but it was a close thing.

Then, three or four of James's hives of bees swarmed, and no matter how fast he ran after them, banging a spoon against a plate to encourage them to return, they flew over the woods and out of sight for ever.

It was a very bad month and everyone on the farm began to go around with faces as long as a wet day.

"It's bad luck we're having," said James.

"It's more than just bad luck, if you ask me," said his wife seriously. "I think it's witchcraft!"

"Witchcraft? What are you talking about? Who ever heard of witches in these parts?"

But James's wife was serious. She crossed herself, and then spoke in a low and quiet voice, slowly at first and then getting quicker as she warmed to what she was saying.

"Remember that strange old woman you met at the cave by the top meadow? Didn't you say that she had one white eye? Well, I believe that was a sign of evil. I think that she has put the Evil Eye on us – she's bewitched us – and if things go on as they are doing, we shall all be dead before long!"

For a moment she was silent, and then she let out a little sob of fear and buried her face in her apron to hide her tears.

After that James too began to think, and the more he thought the more he agreed with what his wife had said. But his heart sank for all that. It was all very well to believe, even to know, that they were bewitched; the problem was to know how to rid themselves of the spell. He went to bed that night with a very heavy heart.

When he woke up next morning it was not to the usual sounds of cheerful bustle about the farmhouse. All he could hear was his wife sobbing downstairs in the kitchen. James flung on his clothes and ran down to see what had happened to upset her. He burst into the kitchen and immediately stopped short: the air was full of a sweet, sickly smell. It seemed thick and heavy and, in spite of himself, he put his hand to his mouth and yawned. For some strange reason he suddenly felt sleepy.

His wife's sobs roused him again. He shook his head

43

in bewilderment and looked around. She was standing by the kitchen table, rubbing at her eyes as if she had woken up only a short time ago. The maid was asleep in a chair by the fire and there, stretched out on the kitchen table and also fast asleep, was his son William.

"What's going on?" yawned James. At his words the maid stirred sleepily and got up, rubbing her eyes. "What's that smell?" went on the farmer.

"It's William!" sobbed his wife. "He's bewitched, I know he is! Look, see how deeply he sleeps. I've tried everything and nothing seems to rouse him!"

"That sickly smell is awful," groaned James. "Open the windows! Open the back door!" He himself threw open a window and noticed idly as he did so that a grey and white spotted butterfly, which had been resting on the woodwork, flew out into the fresh air.

Gradually the sickly smell disappeared, but the boy William still kept on sleeping. They carried him upstairs to his bed and tried to rouse him with both hot and cold drinks, but he still slept. His face was white and drawn and it twitched from time to time as if he were having a bad dream. When James tenderly lifted one of the boy's eyelids, he saw the eyeball rolling wildly about. His breathing was quick and irregular. This was certainly no ordinary sleep!

At that moment there came a loud hammering at the front of the house. In rushed their nearest neighbour, bursting with news.

"James! James! Come quickly. Your fences are all down and your herds and flocks are running!"

James rushed outside and shaded his eyes against the brightness of the rising sun. Over towards the top meadow he could just see that a great length of hedge and fence had been flattened as if a giant had trodden it down. The fields and pastures were empty of animals. His livestock must be scattered all over the countryside!

"Look to the boy," he said grimly to his wife, and then he was gone.

It was nightfall before he came back again, tired and hungry, and scratched and bleeding from the brambles. But with the help of his friends and neighbours he had managed to round up most of the animals and had also rebuilt the fences. When he had eaten he sat at the table, rough hand supporting his chin and deep in thought. At last he spoke.

"Wife, I have been thinking and I have come up with a very curious thought. What living creature was in the house when our boy fell asleep?" He looked towards the stairs, at the top of which the boy still lay in a disturbed sleep.

"Living creatures? Why there were none, James, save you and me."

"Wrong, woman. There was one. I saw it. Answer me this, then. What living creature was up by the cave after I ordered that old woman with the white eye off my land?"

"I can't remember you saying anything about a creature at all."

"Then your memory is not as good as mine. What creature was it, then, that flew into my eyes and nearly made me fall into the animal pit-trap?"

"Oh, I remember that, James. It was a butterfly!"

"Yes, a butterfly. A grey and white spotted butterfly. And that same butterfly has been about whenever trouble has struck!"

"What are you thinking, James?"

"I'm thinking that some witches have cats, and it is said that some witches can change into cats – and into other creatures too! I believe that this white-eyed witch has changed into a butterfly to do her evil work!"

He said no more, but when next morning dawned fine he got up, kissed his wife and sleeping son and prepared to go out. Into his deep pocket he put a fine-meshed net,

45

such as he used for snaring rabbits. Then he said a brief prayer and set off to work.

That day he was to cart logs for firewood from the forest to the farm. He spent most of the morning making slow and heavy journeys along the rutted track in his small cart. His shaggy horse heaved and strained to pull the heavy logs. James appeared to be thinking of nothing but the work, yet all the time he was watching and waiting.

And then it happened! As he walked beside the cart, driving the horse along the track by the river, a grey and white butterfly fluttered into the horse's face. The startled animal reared, whinnying, tipping the logs off the cart over towards where James was walking!

If the logs had landed on top of him they would have broken a limb, or even killed him. But James had been ready for this and he saw the butterfly in time. So, as the horse reared, he leapt. The next second he had taken the net from his pocket and pinned the butterfly underneath.

The insect fluttered wildly under the mesh, and James raised his hand as if to squash it flat. Then he lowered it again. Deftly he tied the sides of the net together and held it up. "There, my beauty!" he said grimly. "If you really are the witch, then we shall soon know. They tell me that witches aren't too keen on water." And so saying he hurled the net into the swift-flowing river.

As it fell, James thought he heard a wild scream. And then as the net began to sink below the surface he saw the butterfly. For a second it seemed to be trying to squeeze through the mesh, but the holes were too small. Then, even as he watched, the insect turned into a white-eyed old woman, the very same one who had been at the cave on the day when all his misfortunes began!

At last the net burst open and the old woman struggled free in the water. Her face was scratched and bleeding from the mesh, and her eyes were frantic. It seemed as though

the cold water was burning her. She screamed with fear and rage.

"I told you to stay off my land!" yelled James.

The witch ceased struggling, but then, as James had guessed would happen, the current carried her to the opposite bank, and although she was swept under the water once or twice she finally managed to scramble out. She sat in a huddled heap on the bank, trembling and defeated.

The farmer called out to her again. "Now clear off out of this place, and don't come back again! Next time I shall squash you flat like the wretched creature you are!" And so saying he strode back to his work.

The old woman was seen only once more and then by a neighbour's child, who reported seeing her running and then hobbling, dripping wet, towards the far hills, muttering to herself.

As for James, he lived the rest of his life in great happiness. His son William had woken from the bewitched sleep at the very moment when the witch had landed in the river. On that day also the dry cow began to yield rich milk again. However, from that time onwards James never saw a butterfly without remembering the beautiful guise the witch had used to work her magic.